from,

Granny Mies.

First published 1982
Second impression 1983
The Hamlyn Publishing Group Limited
London · New York · Sydney · Toronto
Astronaut House, Feltham, Middlesex, England

ISBN 0 600 36668 5

These stories first appeared in *The Enid Blyton
Pennant Series* published in 1950 by Macmillan &
Co. Limited.

Printed in Italy

The runaway cows

and other stories

Enid Blyton

Illustrated by Val Biro

Hamlyn
London·New York·Sydney·Toronto

Contents

Melia's moneybox

Melia was one of five children. She was the middle one of the five. There was nine-year-old Jack, eight-year-old Fanny, seven-year-old Melia, and the six-year-old twins, Alice and Dick.

'I'm Melia the middle one,' Melia told visitors, and that made them laugh. 'Melia Middle,' they said, and kissed her because she was such a jolly, smiling little girl.

One day Granpa arrived with a present for everyone. 'Moneyboxes!' he said, and he gave one to each of his grandchildren. They were sweet. They were like little houses and you had to put the coin in at the wide chimneypot. Each house had the name of its owner painted on it.

9

'There you are!' said Granpa, giving each child one. 'It's time you all learnt to save some of your money. You must put aside a bit for a rainy day, you know.'

'Well, I don't want to spend money on a rainy day,' said Melia. 'Mummy doesn't often let me go out when it's pouring with rain.'

That made Granpa laugh. He told Melia that putting money away for a rainy day meant saving up in case you suddenly had to buy something you didn't expect.

'Grown-ups save money in case somebody is ill and they have to pay for doctors and medicines,' said Granpa. 'Children should learn to save up too—they should buy birthday presents for their mothers and fathers, and things like that.'

The children liked their moneyboxes. It was fun to pop coins into
the chimney and hear them fall with
a crash. You could get them out by
___ing a trapdoor with a key, at
___ bottom of the house.

___ said Granpa, 'I am goin

to take you all to the zoo in a few weeks' time, and I want you to save up for it. I shall double any money you have in your moneyboxes when the time comes—so if you want elephant rides and things like that, you had better save hard. We will

see who is the best at saving.'

The children began to save. 'If I save £2 and Granpa doubles it, I shall have £4 to spend at the zoo!' said Jack, and he put into the box every 5p and 10p coin that anyone gave him.

Melia managed to save 25p, and then she heard that Benny, a little friend of hers, was very ill. She was sad for him, and she unlocked her moneybox and took out 20p. That only left 5p inside. She bought a bunch of sweet peas and took it round to Benny.

'The smell makes me feel better,' he said; 'you **are** kind, Melia.'

'You're silly,' said Jack, when he heard about it. 'Now you've only got 5p left.'

But soon Melia had 55p inside, because Auntie Rose came and gave everyone something to spend. How the moneyboxes clinked!

Then Melia's teacher at school told them about a poor old woman she knew who had no money to buy herself some spectacles. She had broken hers, and could not see

to read or sew. She asked the children if they could each spare 5p to help the old woman to buy her glasses.

Melia rushed home and emptied her moneybox. She took all the 55p to her teacher. 'Here you are,' she said, 'give her all this. I'm so sorry for that poor old woman.'

So that meant Melia had to start all over again. Even the twins had more money in their boxes than Melia. It was silly of Melia, Jack said, to keep giving away all her money.

'Well—I really will try to save now,' said Melia. She didn't buy any sweets. She didn't buy the doll's shoes she saw in the toyshop. She didn't buy anything at all.

Then she had almost 50p in her box, and she felt pleased. It was hard save up money, and give up gs she wanted, but it felt nice to she had something in her ox.

Then Granny fell down and broke her leg! All the children were sad, because they loved little old Granny. 'If Granpa didn't want us to save our money, I'd buy her some flowers,' said Jack.

'He might be cross if we opened our moneyboxes so near the time when he's taking us to the zoo,' said Fanny.

'Granny's got plenty of flowers in her own garden,' said the twins, who didn't want to open their moneyboxes just when they were getting so full. 'She doesn't need any more flowers.''

Only Melia said nothing. She did love little old Granny so much. A broken leg must hurt. Perhaps Granny would never be able to walk any more. Melia couldn't bear it.

'I won't buy flowers, because they ⌐ say Granny has plenty,' she ⌐ght, 'but I just **must** take her a

present. I like presents when I'm ill. I'm sure Granny does too. Oh dear —and I was trying so hard to save up too. But Granny's broken leg is more important than my savings!' Melia opened her moneybox and took out all the money. 'You're a naughty girl,' said Jack. 'Granpa will be cross with you, always spending your money like that. What are you going to do with it?'

27

Melia didn't like to tell him. Jack would laugh at her, she felt sure. She was going to spend all her money on some special peppermints that Granny loved! Off she went and bought a whole bagful.

Granny was so pleased. She hugged Melia and said, 'Well, Miss Kind-Heart; if that isn't just like you!'

Two days later Granpa arrived to take them all to the zoo. 'Now then,' he said, rattling the money in his pocket. 'Open up your money-boxes, and I'll double all you've got there! You must each pay all your own fares and rides and tea, because I shall double your money.'

Jack had £2. Fanny had £1·65. The twins had £1·12 each.

'And what about Melia?' said Granpa, as he paid out lots of money to the others.

'My box is empty,' said Melia, and she went red. 'I'm sorry, Granpa. I'm no good at saving. Things keep happening that make me spend my money. I'll have to stay at home.'

31

'Oh no, you won't,' said Granpa, and he took Melia on his knee. 'Here's a little girl who can teach all you others the right way to save and spend money! She saved it up because she wanted to go to the zoo as you all did—but when Benny was ill she made him happy with a toy bought out of her money.

'And she gave her teacher all her savings for the old woman who wanted new glasses. And then, when she had saved up again, Granny broke her leg, and Melia was the only one who thought Granny more important than her money, and spent every penny of it to cheer her up.'

Nobody said a word. They all

suddenly felt rather mean. 'Melia,' said Granpa, 'I'm proud of you! It's good to save money—but it's better to spend it the right way when you have to. You know how to save —and you know how to spend. I shall give you £5 for yourself to spend at the zoo. Come along.'

So off they all went—and how happy Melia was as she skipped along by her Granpa. He hadn't laughed at her. He hadn't scolded her. He had understood that she had to be kind and generous with her money as well as careful to save it up. Dear old Granpa.

I think Melia was right, don't you? It's good to save, but it's even better to be kind when you see the chance.

The runaway cows

Tom, Dick, Harry and Will were coming home from school one day, when they saw five red and white cows walking down the road.

'Look at those cows!' said Tom. 'All by themselves! They must have got out of the field and run away.'

'They belong to Farmer White,' said Dick. 'Won't he be wild?'

'We'd better tell him,' said Harry.

'No, we won't,' said Will. 'He's a horrid man. He shouts at boys and girls. And you know he won't let

anyone go blackberrying in that field where the hedges are simply covered with big blackberries.'

'So we won't bother about his old cows,' said Tom. 'We'll let them run right away, and perhaps be knocked down by cars.'

'That's not right,' said Dick at once. 'Why should we let the cows come to harm just because we don't like the farmer? You're always saying things like that, Tom.'

'Well, anyway, why should we bother?' said Will lazily. 'It's not our business. They're not our cows. Nobody can make us go and tell the farmer they are loose.'

'That's just it,' said Harry. 'Nobody can make us—it isn't our business—but if **some**body doesn't take some trouble about those cows, they'll be hurt. We ought to make it our job to see they aren't.'

'Well, all I say is, I hope that horrid farmer's cows do get hurt,' said Tom, who was spiteful. 'I'm going home.'

'And I jolly well won't bother
myself to go out of my way to tell
the farmer,' said Will. 'I want my
tea.' So he went home with Tom.

Dick and Harry looked at one another. They were both sensible boys who liked animals and would not let them get hurt if they could help it.

'It's true we don't like Farmer White,' said Harry, 'but all the same we ought to go and tell him. I'll go, Dick, and you chase after the cows and try and head them back.'

So Dick chased after the cows and managed to turn them back up the road again, whilst Harry went to tell the farmer.

He was having his tea. 'What's up?' he said, when he saw Harry.

'Five of your cows are loose on the road, sir,' said Harry. 'I've sent Dick to turn them back, but perhaps you had better come and take them to their field. Dick isn't very used to cows.'

'Thanks,' said the farmer, getting up. 'It's nice to see a boy who'll take the trouble to put things right without being asked to! I'll come now.'

47

They went out and soon met Dick with the cows. He had found a stick and was feeling quite important chasing the cows back to the farm.

'Good of you to trouble,' said the farmer. 'I must find out who left my gate open. Just go ahead and see if it's shut or open now, will you?'

It was open. 'There you are!' said the farmer crossly. 'Some silly boy left it open, I suppose, in spite of the notice on it, PLEASE SHUT THIS GATE. Well—I should think all boys were silly and tiresome if you hadn't given me your help today. Thank you.'

'Very pleased to help you,' said Dick politely. Just as they were going, the farmer turned back and shouted.

'Hi! Do you like blackberries?'

'Oh yes!' said both the boys.

'Well, there are some fine ones on the hedge in that field over there,' said the farmer, pointing with his finger. 'You and your friend can go and pick them whenever you like. I won't let other boys into the field because they leave the gates open.'

'Oh, **thanks**!' said Dick and Harry in delight. Goodness—they would be able to take big baskets home full of ripe blackberries to-morrow.

'What a bit of luck!' said Harry,

as they went home. 'Weren't Tom and Will silly not to come and help with the cows too?'

The next day the two boys went to get the blackberries. They filled two big baskets and took them home.

On the way back they met Tom and Will. How the boys stared when they saw the enormous blackberries.

'We got them in the field over there,' said Dick, pointing.

'You're not allowed to go there,' said Will at once.

'Yes, we are. The farmer said we could,' said Dick, and told Will and Tom all that had happened the day before.

'You might take us with you tomorrow,' said Tom. Harry shook his head.

'No,' he said. 'You wouldn't help yesterday, Tom, and we did. We didn't expect a reward, of course, but it was nice to get one. If you'd helped, you would have shared. As it is, the farmer said that only Dick and I were to go.'

'Well, I shall help next time!' said Tom, looking ashamed. 'I'm glad the cows weren't hurt. You deserve the blackberries, Harry!'

How they enjoyed the blackberry tarts their mothers made—but they did deserve a treat didn't they?

Stones for a donkey

'Hey, Tom, go and fetch my donkey and take him up the hill to Mrs. Brown's,' shouted the farmer. 'She has got some washing to send back to my wife, and the donkey can bring it.'

'Right, sir,' said Tom, and went to fetch the little grey donkey. He was a fat little animal, good-natured and strong. Tom soon got him out of the field, jumped on his back and rode him away.

Now, it was winter-time. The roads had frozen in the night, and they were very slippery indeed. It was all right for the donkey so long as he was on the level road, but as soon as he began to climb the hill, his hooves began to slip.

'Come on, now, come on!' said Tom, who was an impatient boy. 'Get along there!'

The donkey tried again, but his feet slipped badly, and he was afraid of falling over. So he stood still.

Tom hit him with a stick. 'Will you get on, you stupid creature? How am I to get to the top of the hill and back if you stand still like this?'

The donkey would not move.

61

Tom got off and tried to push him
up the hill. But the donkey wouldn't
budge. He wasn't going to fall down
and break his leg if he could help it!

By the side of the road there were heaps of small stones. Tom felt cross, and he went to the stones. He picked up a handful and threw them hard at the donkey. They hit him on his back and made him jump. He started forward a step or two.

'Ha! That makes you move!' cried Tom, pleased. He picked up another handful of the stones and flung them with all his might. The poor little donkey was hurt in a dozen places, and brayed loudly.

'Move on, I tell you, move on!' shouted Tom, but the donkey would not go for more than one or two steps. So Tom threw more and more stones at him, getting angrier and angrier.

A smaller boy came up the hill and looked at Tom. 'Those stones are hurting the donkey,' he said. 'Do stop throwing them at the poor thing. Can't you see he is afraid of moving on because his feet slip?'

'Oh, he's just stupid, that's all,' said Tom. 'And don't you interfere with me, or I'll throw stones at you too!'

'Shall I help you?' said the boy, not taking any notice of Tom's angry voice.

'How can you help me?' said Tom roughly. 'It's only these stones that will get the donkey to move.'

'Yes, you're right,' said the boy. 'But I could use the stones in quite a different way to make him move. Shall I show you?'

Tom nodded. He felt sure that no way of using the stones would make the donkey move on, except the way he himself had used—throwing a handful as hard as he could.

'I live just here,' said the boy, pointing to a house. 'I won't be a minute. I'm going to get something.'

He ran to a shed beside the house and came out with a small spade. Tom was surprised. What did he want a spade for?

The boy began to dig into the heaps of small stones by the road-side, and he spread them in front of the donkey, making a path of stones for him to walk on.

'You see, the road here is terribly slippery,' explained the boy in his gentle voice. 'Horses and donkeys are always falling down on this steep bit, and breaking their legs. So these heaps of small pebbles are placed here for people to scatter in front of their animals.'

'Oh,' said Tom, suddenly feeling stupid and small.

'It's no good expecting an animal to go on if it cannot get a firm hold with its feet,' said the boy, busy shovelling hard. 'Better to help it, than to hinder it, don't you think so?'

'Yes,' said Tom.

'Now,' said the boy, 'we'll see what the donkey says about things this time. Come along, old fellow.

Walk on the stones, and you'll be all right.'

The donkey put out a foot and felt the stones, which gave him a good grip on the slippery road. He walked a few steps over the scattered pebbles, and went safely up the very steep piece.

'There you are!' said the boy.
'Now he'll be all right, I think.
Anyway, there are little heaps of
pebbles beside any very steep bit,
so you'll know what to do another
time.'

73

'Thanks,' said Tom, and went on up the hill with the donkey. He thought hard. He had been stupid, but that boy had been clever. He had been unkind, but that boy had had pity on the donkey. He had tried to force the donkey on by cruelty, but that boy had helped it on with kindness.

'I don't think much of myself,' thought Tom, ashamed. 'Poor little donkey!'

'Hee-haw!' said the donkey, looking round at Tom. 'Hee-haw! There are two ways of using stones! Just remember that, Tom! And there are two ways of doing anything, the good way and the bad way. Hee-haw!'

The princess and the cottage-girl

Anna often saw the little Princess Peronel walking in the woods with her nurse. She stood and watched her.

Peronel was pretty. She had lovely clothes. She had a pony of her own. She had a car to go riding in. She had the most lovely food, Anna was sure.

'I don't like Peronel,' said Anna
to herself. She was jealous of the
little princess, and if she could have
smacked her, she would.

'She's got so many things and I
haven't anything at all!' thought
Anna. 'I hate her!'

80

One day the princess came run-
ing by Anna all alone. For the first
time she had no one with her. She
stopped by Anna and laughed.
'What do you think?' she said. 'My
nurse is asleep and I have run away
and left her. Shall we have a game?'

Anna did not smile. She looked at the princess's fine clothes with envy, and then she looked down at her rough red dress.

'I don't want to play with you,' she said rudely, to Peronel. 'You've got all the luck and I haven't any! You're a princess and I am only a cottage-girl.'

'Surely you don't think I'm lucky to be a princess!' cried Peronel in surprise. 'What—lucky to have to go out always with a nurse, never alone! Lucky to have to sit for hours and hours at dull parties where there's much too much to eat and drink! Lucky to have a father and mother who are so busy being a king and queen that they haven't time to tuck me up at night!'

'Well, you don't think I'm lucky to be a poor little cottage-girl, do you?' said Anna. 'I have to mind our baby. I have to live in a poky little room, and share my bed with my little sister. I have to work in the fields with my father. I have to help my mother to bake cakes.'

'Oh, how lovely!' said Peronel. 'Our palace cook is far too grand even to let me peep in the kitchen. I say—we're awfully alike, aren't we? Shall we change places for a bit? You be me, and I'll be you! Do!'

It wasn't a bit of good saying no
to Peronel. Before Anna knew what
was happening, she was in Peronel's
clothes and Peronel was in hers.
Peronel danced off to Anna's cottage
to find the baby. She loved babies
and there was none at the palace.

86

Peronel's nurse appeared, hot and angry. She saw Anna and thought she was the princess. 'You naughty little girl! How dare you run away?' she cried. 'You will have dry bread for tea and no cake at all!' Anna was taken off to the palace. The nurse was very, very strict, much stricter than Anna's mother. She nagged at Anna all the time. 'Elbows off the table! Don't talk with your mouth full! What **have** you done to your hair? Is this the way for a princess to behave? I shall report you to the queen, your mother!'

When the queen came in to pay a hurried visit to the princess, the nurse gave her a very bad report.

'How naughty you are!' said the

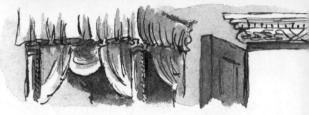

queen. 'Don't you know how important it is for a princess to learn all these things? Nurse, see that Peronel is made ready to attend a big party tonight—but you understand, Peronel, you mustn't eat anything except your milk pudding, because the other food would upset you.'

The nurse bathed and dressed Anna. She scolded all the time. 'Stand up straight. Now, let me see if you can curtsy nicely. Good gracious, child, you did that as if you had never curtsied in your life before!'

Anna couldn't help looking forward to the party—but oh, how dull
it was! It lasted for hours, and most
of the time Anna had to sit quite
still, or have her hand kissed by a
lot of old gentlemen she didn't like.
Then, at the banquet, she was not
allowed to have any of the beautiful
food on the table.

93

'Just your milk pudding, dear,'
whispered the nurse.

'I want some jelly!' said Anna
loudly. The queen was shocked.

'Take her to bed,' she said. 'She
must be tired.'

94

So Anna was hustled away,
scolded and put to bed. She cried.
The queen didn't come to say
goodnight. The nurse gave her a
peck on the cheek and that was all.
Anna was lonely.

'I don't like being a princess,' she
thought. 'It isn't much fun after all.
Peronel must have had a dull time.
I'm going home and Peronel will
have to come back.'

So she slipped out of bed and
dressed. She climbed out of the
window and ran through the palace
grounds. She came at last to her
own little cottage. She climbed up
the old apple-tree outside her bed-
room window and tapped Peronel
on the shoulder.

Peronel awoke. She was lying cuddled up to Anna's little fat sister. She sat up.

'I've come back,' said Anna. 'You dress quickly and go back to the palace.'

'I don't want to,' said Peronel

at once. 'I simply love your home.
I think that your mother is the nicest
woman I ever knew. Do you know,
she took me on her knee tonight and
told me a story?'

'She always does that,' said
Anna. 'Quick, get up.'

'And she came and tucked me up and kissed me goodnight,' said Peronel. 'And I do so love your little baby. I wish I could look after him all day. And your little fat sister here loves me. We are going blackberrying tomorrow. That will be fun.'

'No, you're not,' said Anna. 'Do get up.'

'Anna, your father is so nice too,' said Peronel. 'He gave me the top of his egg at teatime. **My** father never did that.'

'Well—my father always does,' said Anna. 'We take it in turn to have the top of his egg. Peronel, **will** you get up?'

'And I love your cosy kitchen,'
said the little princess. 'You've no
idea how warm and comfortable
and homey it was this evening. A
palace is never homey. Anna, I do
beg and beg of you to change places
with me and let me stay here with
your darling mother and little baby
brother and sister. Anna, do.'

'No,' said Anna. 'Get up.'

'But, Anna, you said you were jealous of me, you said I was lucky to be a princess—well, I'm telling you that you can be lucky too, if you want to,' said Peronel. 'Don't you **want** to be a princess?'

'No,' said Anna, 'I don't. I was silly to be jealous. I just made myself unhappy, and I hated you, when all the time you were a nice little girl I'd like to play with. It's no fun being something you weren't meant to be. I want to come back home.'

'All right,' said Peronel, with a sigh. 'I didn't really think you'd want to give up this cosy little home, with your nice mother and father. How I'd love them! Anna, will you let me come and nurse your baby some time, if I can slip away from my nurse?'

'Yes,' said Anna. 'And you can come and play with me, because I like you very much. I was silly and horrid and stupid. Jealousy is a nasty thing—it makes you see things all wrong.'

'I'm not jealous of **you**,' said Peronel, 'but I do think you're lucky, Anna, I do, I do. Let's be friends, shall we?'

So they are. They play together when they can, and Peronel nurses the baby as often as she is allowed to. Anna isn't jealous any more—she knows that if she is, Peronel will only be too glad to change places with her again!

The boy who found tenpence

One day Benny was walking along the road and saw something glittering in the gutter.

'Oh!' said Benny happily. 'It's a silver coin! Fancy finding tenpence! Today must be my lucky day.'

He picked up the money. What should he buy with it? 'I know!' he said, 'I'll buy a new trowel for my garden.'

Benny had a little garden of his own, and he grew flowers and lettuces and radishes in it. He was really a clever little gardener. It would be nice to buy a new trowel to dig with. His old one was broken.

Benny put the tenpence into his pocket. He didn't stop to think that somebody must have lost it. He didn't try to find out who it was— but he soon knew.

Coming back down the road was
a little girl. Benny knew her quite
well. It was Sally who lived round
the corner. She was a dear little girl
and Benny often played with her.

Sally was crying. She dabbed her
eyes with her hanky, and then
looked down at the ground. Then
she dabbed her eyes again. She was
looking for something.

Benny knew what it was, of course. Sally was looking for the tenpence he had found. But he didn't say anything about it at all.

'Oh, Benny,' said Sally, wiping her eyes. 'I've lost my tenpence. Mummy sent me shopping with it. She told me to buy a lettuce for dinner—and I lost the tenpence.'

'Oh,' said Benny.

'And . Mummy will scold me dreadfully, and call me a baby,' said poor Sally. 'I do so hope I find it. I'm looking very hard.'

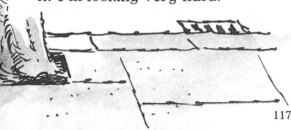

Sally went on down the road, looking everywhere for the tenpence that was in Benny's pocket. Benny knew she would never find it. He knew he ought to give it back to her. But he did so much want that new trowel.

He ran to the shop that sold trowels and bought a fine one for tenpence. It had a small handle, just big enough for his hand to hold. What a lot of gardening he would do with his new trowel!

'I shall dig with it this afternoon,' he said. 'I shall have a very happy time.'

But Benny didn't feel very happy when he dug in his garden that day. He kept thinking of Sally's tear-wet face. He kept wondering if Sally's mother had scolded her—perhaps even smacked her and sent her to bed.

Sally was such a dear little girl.

She always shared her sweets with
Benny. She often asked him to tea.
She always played the games he
wanted to play.

The tea-bell rang and Benny
went in to wash his dirty hands, and
brush his hair. Mummy was at the
table, waiting for him.

'Did you have a nice time in the garden?' she said. 'I have been out for a walk. I met little Sally Jones. She was very sad, because her mother was cross with her for losing tenpence this morning. She was still looking for it when I met her.'

Benny went very red. He felt miserable. He didn't like to think of Sally still looking for tenpence she would never find.

'I suppose someone must have found it,' said Mummy.

'Well, finding is keeping, isn't it, Mummy?' said Benny.

'Of course not,' said his mother in surprise. 'That's a very dishonest thing to say, Benny. You know perfectly well that if **you** found anything in the road, you would bring it to me at once, and we would try to find out who had lost it.'

Benny went redder than ever. He looked at his mother, and he felt so dreadful that he knew he must tell her what he had done, even if she was cross with him and ashamed.

'Mummy,' he said, 'I found that tenpence of Sally's. It was in the gutter. I picked it up.'

'Well, why didn't you say so before?' said Mummy. 'Now you can go and give it back to her. Little

Sally will be so pleased.'

'But I can't,' wailed Benny. 'I've spent it. I bought a new trowel with it.'

'Oh, Benny—no wonder you keep going red, and looking so miserable,' said Mummy. 'You must have been a very unhappy little boy today.'

'I am,' said Benny. 'I wish I hadn't spent that tenpence. I haven't even a penny in my moneybox, so I can't give Sally anything back. She was going to buy a lettuce with the tenpence. She told me so.'

'Well—you have lettuces growing in your garden,' said Mummy at once. Benny's face grew a bit brighter.

'Oh!' he said. 'Do you think it would put things right if I took Sally round one of my lettuces, Mummy? I could choose the very nicest.'

'It would make Sally happy, and make you feel a bit happier too,' said Mummy. 'But you mustn't forget that you have made Sally very sad today. You ought to give her something to make up for that.'

'Yes, I ought,' said Benny. 'I'll go and get a basket and get the things now.' So Benny cut two big lettuces from his garden, a bunch of red radishes, and a lovely bunch of flowers. He put them into his basket and ran round to Sally with them.

'Sally!' he said. 'I found your tenpence, and I spent it. I'm very, very sorry. I want to make up for it —so I have brought you these.'

'Oh, thank you, Benny!' said Sally, and she gave him a hug. 'I feel much happier now. Mummy won't be cross with me any more. It wasn't nice of you to spend my tenpence—but it **is** nice of you to make up for it like this, so I like you just as much as ever I did. Will you come to tea tomorrow?'

'Yes, I will,' said Benny, pleased. 'I'll never keep things I find again, Sally—I did feel so unhappy!'

The wonderful conjurer

The boys in Mr. Brown's school were excited. Ricardo, the great conjurer, was coming to the town hall the next week, to do some conjuring.

'I hope we can go,' said Alan.

131

'Mr. Brown hasn't been in a very good temper lately. He keeps saying what a rude and ill-mannered lot of boys we are.'

'Well—he always says that,' said Dick. 'I expect he will let us go.'

But Mr. Brown said no, not one boy in his class should have Wednesday afternoon off to go and see Ricardo, the wonderful conjurer!

'When you learn a few more manners, you shall have a few more treats,' he said. 'Once again I have had a complaint from someone in the town, who says that a boy wearing the cap of our school bumped into her in the road, upset her bag and rushed off without saying he was sorry. Stand up, the boy who did that.'

Nobody stood up. 'There you are, you see!' said Mr. Brown. 'The rude boy is a little coward as well. There's another thing too—I hear that there is a lot of pushing when some of you try to get on to the bus. No need for that. Get on when your turn comes. I never had such a bad-mannered class in my life!'

The boys went out gloomily. 'It's mean of him, said Alan. 'He might let us off to see Ricardo. I'd love to see him.'

'Well—I suppose it's our own fault,' said Tom, the head-boy of the class. 'Some of us do behave badly in the street. It does let the school down. For goodness' sake don't let Mr. Brown have any more complaints from anyone, or he'll be making us miss cricket or something.'

'What about trying a spot of good manners and politeness?' said Lennie. 'Then maybe Mr. Brown would let us go.'

'He wouldn't,' said Alan. 'People don't write to him about good

manners, they only complain about bad ones. He'd never hear if we suddenly turned over a new leaf.'

They went home. Alan had to wait for a bus. He got on, remembering not to push. He found a seat and sat down. At the next stop a lot more people got on. Alan saw some of them standing up.

He remembered what his mother had often said. 'Alan, I'm always proud of a boy who gives others his seat, or helps an old lady, or gives a hand anywhere. I always hope my own boy will do that, when I see others being good-mannered and kind.'

So Alan, who liked doing what his mother said, got up and offered his seat to a white-haired man with piercing black eyes.

'Thanks, old son,' said the man, and sat down. 'Nice to see a boy with good manners.'

Another day, as he went to afternoon school, Alan saw an old lady waiting to cross the road. Buses and cars went by and she seemed afraid to go.

Alan felt shy, but he knew he ought to help if he could. He went up to her and raised his cap.

'Can I help you across?' he said.

'Well—my son is just coming,' said the very old lady. 'But you can take me across if you like. Thank you very much.'

So Alan took her across, and when she was safely on the other side, a white-haired man with very dark eyes came running over the road. 'Thanks!' he said to Alan. 'I was afraid my old mother might

cross without me, as I had to keep
her waiting. Hallo—aren't you the
boy who gave me his seat the other
day?'

'Yes,' said Alan. 'I remember you.'

'Nice sort of fellow, aren't you?' said the man. 'What school do you go to?'

'Mr. Brown's,' said Alan.

'Ah—some of his boys are going to see the show at the town hall tomorrow, aren't they?' said the man. Alan wondered how he knew.

'Yes,' he said, 'but not my class, unluckily. Mr. Brown says we're so bad-mannered he won't give us any treats at the moment.'

'Well, well—that **is** a pity!' said the man, and went off with his old mother.

Alan went to school the next day. It was the day of the conjuring

show. The boys who were going were all talking about it in excitement.

'He gets goldfish out of the air!' said Harry.

'He makes a huge big flag come out of his mouth!' said Peter.

Mr. Brown's class were very gloomy. They didn't want to listen, but they had to.

A note arrived for Mr. Brown in the middle of the dictation class. He opened it and read it, looking very surprised. Then he knocked on his desk with his hand.

'Boys! I have an interesting letter here. I will read what it says, and I am sure you will be as surprised as I am.

143

144

' "Dear Mr. Brown,

I would like to tell you that one of your boys gave up his seat to me in a bus the other day, and the next day he took my old mother safely across the road. It is pleasant to meet a boy with courtesy and good manners. I hear that his class are not to go to my show this afternoon, but I would like to say that if you would allow them to, I would be pleased to give them all free tickets, in return for the pleasure that one boy's good manners gave me.

Yours faithfully,
Ricardo the Conjurer!" '

The boys leapt up and cheered.
'Can we go, sir? Do say we can.
Hurrah!'

'Wait,' said Mr. Brown, knocking
on his desk again. 'Wait. Who is this
boy who has won this treat for his
class by his politeness and good

manners? You should thank him.
What a pleasant change it is to have
a note like this instead of endless
complaints of rudeness! I want to
know who this boy is.'

It was easy to pick him out. Alan
was red as a beetroot, and the boys
soon saw it.

'It's old Alan! Good old Alan! I bet you didn't know this was going to happen when you gave up your seat, Alan.'

'Of course I didn't,' said Alan. 'It's a very little thing to do. I think Mr. Ricardo is jolly decent.'

Everyone thought so too. 'We'll write and thank him after his show,' said Lennie, and Mr. Brown beamed at him.

'My word, you'll learn a few good manners yet!' he said, pleased. 'Well, you can go, of course. I hope you enjoy it.'

They did—and it was quite true
about the goldfish. The conjurer
did take some out of the air. He gave
one of them to Alan after the show,
and Alan has still got it in a bowl.
Wasn't he lucky?

The little girl
who was afraid

Molly was a funny little girl, so shy and afraid of everyone that the other children laughed at her.

'She's a cowardy-custard!' said Joan. 'If she met a goose she couldn't say "Boo" to it. She'd run away.'

'She squeals if she sees a spider,' said John.

'She ran home crying yesterday because my puppy jumped up at her and asked her to play with him,' said Donald.

'She's even afraid of the scare-crow in the field,' said Kenneth. 'She won't go near him. I think she's the silliest little girl I know. Let's call her Cowardy-Custard.'

So poor Molly was always called Cowardy-Custard, and she didn't like it a bit. She tried hard not to mind spiders. She tried hard not to be afraid of all the dogs she met.

She even climbed up a tree when the others dared her to, although she was very much afraid of falling. But she did so badly want to be called 'Molly' and not 'Cowardy-Custard'.

Still, the name stuck to her, and Molly had to pretend not to mind, though she often cried in bed about it.

'I know I'm a coward,' she said.
'I know I'm afraid of dogs and cows
and spiders and beetles and climbing

up trees and sliding on the ice. Still, I **might** be better if only the others would help me, instead of laughing at me.'

But the others didn't help her, which was a pity. So Molly still had to hear herself called 'Cowardy-Custard,' and she was afraid she always would.

One Saturday the children thought they would all go for a walk together to see what they could find to bring to school on Monday for the Nature lesson.

'Are you coming too, Cowardy-Custard?' said Joan. Molly nodded. She liked the country, even though it seemed full of dogs and cows and insects she didn't like.

'We'll all meet at the corner of Cuckoo Lane,' said Donald. 'Ten o'clock. Don't be late.'

So at ten o'clock everyone was there, and the children set off happily. There were eleven of them, the whole class. That was fun.

'We ought to find a nice lot of things to take back,' said Kenneth. 'Miss Brown **will** be surprised on Monday to see such a lot of flowers and buds and things for her Nature lesson.'

Kenneth found some primroses and anemones. Joan found an early lords-and-ladies plant, and all the children gathered round to look at its queer purple, poker-like tongue.

John found an old nest in a tree,

and took it out very carefully. 'A chaffinch built this last year,' he said. 'Miss Brown will be pleased with this.'

The children had a very happy morning. On the way back they heard some cows mooing in a field. Molly didn't like the noise at all. The children peeped through a gap in the hedge to see the cows.

'I say! They are all standing round a ditch at the end of the field,' said Harry. 'I believe one of their calves must have fallen in. Let's go and see.'

They went through the gap and
ran to the end of the field. The cows
looked round at them. They had
very big horns, and two of the cows
mooed loudly.

'They are angry about something,' said Joan. 'Don't go too near.'

Molly was afraid. She was just going to run away when she caught sight of something in the ditch. It was the dearest little calf she had ever seen!

It was red and white, it had big brown eyes, and no horns. Molly loved it. Then she saw that its head was caught in some barbed wire.

'Poor little thing,' said Kenneth. 'It must have jumped into the ditch, tried to scramble out the other side, and got its head into the barbed wire. Look, it's bleeding round the neck.'

The calf tried to struggle away from the wire and made a funny moaning noise. 'Don't do that, little calf,' said Joan. 'You'll hurt yourself again.'

'Can't one of you boys go and untwist the wire?' said Molly. 'Don't be afraid of the cows. You always say they won't hurt you.'

'Well—they look a bit fierce this morning,' said Donald. 'And that cow keeps putting her head down as if she wants to toss us.'

Nobody would rescue the poor little calf. It gave such a miserable moan that Molly couldn't bear it. Half crying with fear she went towards the cows. If nobody else would save that little calf, she must.

The cows mooed at her. Two put down their heads and she saw their sharp horns. She stopped. The calf made a crying noise and Molly took another step forward. Then, to her great surprise, the cows moved away and made way for her. The little girl rushed quickly between them and came to the ditch.

Still crying with fear, she un-
twisted the barbed wire, her hands
trembling. The wire scratched her
hands, but she didn't call out.

The little calf was free. It scrambled up the side of the ditch and ran to its mother. The cows looked at Molly and then lumbered away with the calf. The mother cow mooed as if to say thank you.

The other children had watched all this in silence. Molly faced them, tears still running down her cheeks,

for she had been very much afraid
all the time.

'I suppose you're going to laugh
at me now because I cried when I
was so afraid,' she said. 'Well, I
couldn't help being afraid, I couldn't
help being a coward.'

'Molly! You were marvellous!'
said Kenneth at once. 'We were all

afraid—but you were the only one who went to save the calf, in spite of your fear! You were wonderful.'

'You are the very bravest of us all!' said Joan in great surprise. 'You did something you were afraid of doing—but you did it! That's not being a coward, silly—that's being as brave as brave can be!'

'If George had been here **he** would have rescued the calf too,' said Harry, 'but he's not afraid of cows, as you are, so it wouldn't have been nearly as brave a thing to do as you did. You're a kind, brave girl, Molly.'

'We'll never, never call you Cowardy-Custard again,' said John. And they never did.

I think Harry was right, don't
you? It's very brave to do something you are afraid of doing. You
never know how brave you can be
till you try.

We are your friends

Tommy was a little town boy. He raced about the streets, shouted and yelled, chased all the cats he saw, and shooed away the pigeons. He was that sort of boy.

Then one day he went to stay

with his uncle in the country. Uncle George had a farm. He kept cows, sheep, hens, and geese, so it was an exciting place to stay at. He had dogs and cats as well.

Tommy had never seen so many animals and birds in his life. He shouted at them to make them run away. He threw stones to frighten them. He chased them.

The dogs would have bitten him if he hadn't been such a small boy. The cats would have scratched him if they had got near enough. None of the creatures liked Tommy.

'Why is he so cruel to us?' they said to one another. 'We are his friends! What a funny boy to chase us away and shout and throw stones! Doesn't he **know** that we are his friends?'

'Shall we treat him in the same way?' said a cow with big horns. 'I could toss him easily.'

'And I could chase him, and hiss at him and peck him,' said the biggest goose.

'And I wouldn't mind nipping his leg if it would teach him a lesson,' said one of the dogs.

176

'Well,' said a sheep, 'if we did that, it would make him think we were his enemies, not his friends. He would hate us all the more—and hatred is a horrid thing, cruel and cold.'

'It would be better to teach him to love us,' said another cow, mooing softly. 'You see—Tommy is really more foolish than bad. He doesn't

know we are his friends!'

'Well, we will all tell him, then,'
said the biggest dog. 'See, there he is
in the corner of the field. He has
fallen asleep in the sun. Let's go and
talk to him.'

So they all went to where Tommy lay fast asleep. They stood round him in a circle, the big cows outside, the sheep next, the dogs next, the geese next, then the hens and the cats. The biggest cow mooed to wake Tommy.

He opened his eyes and sat up. When he saw all the birds and animals round him, he was very frightened.

'Go away,' he said. 'Have you come to bite me and scratch me and poke me with your horns? Go away! I don't like you, and I'm sure you don't like **me**.'

'Tommy, we are your friends,' mooed the big cow. 'We have come to tell you.'

'Don't be silly,' said Tommy. 'How can you be my friends? You don't do anything for me! You just run about the fields and eat.'

'We do a lot of things for you,' said the cow. 'Why, you could hardly live without us! We give you so very many presents.'

'I don't believe you,' said Tommy.

'Now listen,' said the cow. 'I give you milk each day, and cream. I give you butter for your bread. I give you cheese as well. Don't you think those are lovely presents?'

'And I give you the wool for your warm jerseys and your stockings,' said the sheep. 'The vest you wear is made of my wool too. I keep you warm.'

'And I guard your house,' said the biggest dog. 'I keep foxes away from the chickens. I find any sheep that are lost. I am your guardian, and the sheep's too.'

'And I give you the feathers in your pillow,' said the biggest goose. 'Isn't your pillow soft and warm at night? Well, your aunt filled it with my feathers. That is my present to you.'

183

'And we catch all the mice and rats that steal your food,' said a big tabby cat. 'We work very hard each night. We live round the barns, and we are always watching for your enemies, the mice and the rats.'

'And we lay you eggs for your breakfast and your tea,' said a brown hen in a loud, clucking voice. 'Isn't that a friendly thing to do? Why should you throw stones at us, Tommy, when we lay eggs for you to eat?'

Tommy looked so surprised. 'Do you all do so much for me?' he said, and he felt ashamed. 'Are you really my friends?'

'Well, isn't it a friendly thing to do, to give you so many presents, and to work so hard for you and your family?' said the big dog. 'All we ask in return is a little food and shelter—and some friendliness too. We all like a kind word, or a pat. I know **I** do!'

'I've been silly,' said Tommy, getting up. 'I didn't know you were my friends. Please, I didn't **know**. I'm not a cruel little boy really. I just didn't **know**!'

'Well, couldn't you think a bit and find out before you treat creatures badly?' said the big cow. 'You could listen to what people say, you could read books, you could be wise instead of foolish—and wise people are never cruel. It is only stupid people, or wicked ones who are cruel.'

187

'I'm not wicked—I've been stupid and that has made me do things a cruel person would do,' said Tommy. 'I want to be friends with you now, if you'll let me. I didn't know you did all those things for me.'

'It's a good rule always to be friendly,' said a dog. 'We are— until we know someone is really an enemy. Then we bite. But we are friendly first.'

'I'll be friendly too,' said Tommy. 'I'll come and talk to you each day, and I'll never shout at you, or throw stones. Thank you for telling me everything. I'm glad you are my friends. I want to be yours too.'

So Tommy is friends with all the animals and birds now, and he is much happier ·than before. Wasn't it nice of them to go and tell him they were his friends? They are yours too, of course.